The rain hit Nicky hard as he came out of school and everyone ran. It was screams and running feet all along the street, especially when the thunder started. So it seemed too good to be true when he saw his dad's yellow Mini. But it wasn't his dad's car, nor was it his dad driving and Nicky is suddenly plunged into a terrifying adventure and a frantic race against time.

BERNARD ASHLEY

Your guess is as good as mine

ILLUSTRATED BY DAVID PARKINS

BARN OWL BOOKS

First published in Great Britain 1983
by Julia MacRae Books, Random House,
20 Vauxhall Bridge Road, London SW1V 2SA
This edition first published 2000 by Barn Owl Books
157 Fortis Green Road, London N10 3LX
Barn Owl Books are distributed by
Frances Lincoln

ISBN 1 903015 04 9
A CIP catalogue record for this book
is available from the British Library

Designed and typeset by Douglas Martin Associates
Printed in China

Contents

CHAPTER ONE

Thunder and lightning

Nicky didn't like this feeling one bit. It made him jumpy, this churning over in his stomach all the time and him not knowing why. Before a big game or a Maths test, all right, he expected it then: but not for no reason, not for just this jittery feeling that if he started something he might not finish it: or that something he didn't like was going to happen.

He came out of the school building and looked up at the sky. Perhaps those black clouds that had hung as low as treetops all day had something to do with it. Well, if so, it'd be a good job when it made up its mind to rain. He'd had enough of the jumps.

It had been one of those days all through: nothing normal about it. Games had been called off because of that dark sky over the marshes, Lee was away with something so there were no laughs to be had, and there was nothing to look forward to on the telly that night. He took a deep breath and blew out his disgust. He'd probably end up reading a book! Well, at least someone else's jitters might cheer him up. Yes, tucked up in bed with his spy book – that wouldn't be so bad. Then it'd be switch off the light and hope Lee was back tomorrow.

He looked up into the gloom again, at the

signboard above the school gate. But he wasn't in the mood to jump at it tonight. Let the flaky old paint of *Mrs A. Bottomley* be, for today. There was tomorrow and all the year to wear the letters off at both ends and turn it into a laugh. It wasn't the same fun without Lee and, besides, tonight wasn't a night to hang about.

So, on he went out of the gate and into the street. He brushed his hand half-heartedly into the dusty hedge of the caretaker's garden: but there wasn't even a web, let alone a spider. All the signs seemed to be saying get home fast. It was definitely one of those get-it-over days.

Rachel Power jumped at the board Nicky had passed and followed him out of the school, keeping a safe ten metres behind. She'd catch him up when he was past that spider hedge.

He was usually a good laugh, was Nicky. They'd always walked home together, before Lee came: you just had to look out for his tricks, that was all. Spiders down your neck – and brilliant, he was, at kiss chase.

'Nicky!' she shouted.

But a car came past and he didn't seem to hear. She opened her mouth again. But a cold and sudden plop on the back of her neck put paid to a second shout. An attack of large, splashing drops began hitting the pavement all round her, quickly covering the ground with a pattern of black to match the sky.

She ran. Everyone ran. It was screams and running feet all along the street, especially when the storm began for real. Every head was down, everyone's eyes too busy with the slippery slabs and sudden kerbs to give much thought to what was happening to

anyone else. And Rachel with the rest. She
saw things she wouldn't remember till later,
like lucky Nicky getting a lift in his dad's car
- and something being funny about it and all -
but she didn't take any of it in as she made

her wet dash for home. It was all too drench-
ing for that - and coming in wet and making
work for your mum was something you tried
hard not to do. Against that there wasn't a lot
that really mattered, not Nicky, not funny
cars, not anything . . .

The rain hit Nicky hard, sting, slap, smack around the head, as if he were in a fight with his big brother. There had to be hail in this lot if it was coming down hard enough to hurt, he thought. And was that a rumble of thunder? If it was, there was lightning about, and you could get hurt worse than by hail with all those millions of volts frizzing down. A cold cube of fear suddenly froze up his stomach. That rotten feeling he'd had all day of something bad happening. Was it this? Was it a storm he had to watch out for?

And then he knew. Or he thought he knew. Like some gigantic light being switched on, a wide white flash streaked across the sky. It lit the undersides of things and wiped out every shadow. And in the same stopped heart-beat a crack like something blowing up banged around the streets, shook the sides of houses and rattled at the glass.

Everybody screamed. Everybody ran. And Nicky shouted, certain the thing was meant for him. Everything had been building up to this, then, to him being one of those unlucky ones-in-a-million you read about in the papers. 'Mum! Mum!' In that instant he didn't care who heard him, Rachel Power, little kids . . . He was scared stiff, and he'd never wanted to be safe inside somewhere so badly in all his life.

It seemed too good to be true - when he saw the yellow Mini standing there: his dad having the sense to bring the car round. But his jump for joy lost its heart before his feet got back to the ground. Their Mini was up on blocks in the garden, wasn't it, and this had different rust, and a different number. Same colour, though. Just his rotten luck! A lift home could make all the difference in this storm, where even the rain was that soaking

stuff like a proper shower at the baths – and still hitting him as if it meant it. Nicky put his head down again.

'Quick, get out of this lot! Hop in, son.'

The car door opened, and for a second Nicky was confused. It wasn't their car, he knew that, and yet . . . Why . . . ? He stopped and looked into it.

'Come on, don't hang about. You want to stay out in this storm?'

A man was holding the door open from the inside, respectable looking, smiling just a bit, but with that take-it-or-leave-it look that said it was just a friendly offer in the storm, say yes quick or he'd shut the door and drive off.

Nicky's heart was still thumping with the fright of that sudden flash. Around him the screams and the footsteps had gone as others had shot off to safety somewhere. All he could see at that moment were those four rubber tyres between the man and the road, while in his head he heard his father's words when they'd been caught in the car by a storm. 'You're safe as houses in here, Nicky. We're insulated . . ?

Nicky looked back at the man.

'Quick, then, if you're coming. You know me, don't you? We must live near, I've seen you around.'

Nicky screwed up his eyes in the rain. Now he'd said it, the man did have a face he thought he knew – and he was very smart in a clean, white raincoat, with his shirt collar done up and a tie on.

'Lucky I was passing, with this lot throwing itself down.'

Another flash filled the sky, another bang seemed to shake the car. In the white light the man looked kindly at Nicky, straight, open, not pushing things.

'But I haven't got all day, you know. Anyway, you're wet already and you don't seem to mind the lightning, so perhaps you're not bothered . . .' He started to close the door.

And that made Nicky's mind up. Someone you couldn't trust would have tried a lot harder to get him into the car, wouldn't he? Not only that, now he was dead sure he knew that face.

'Hold on!' Nicky said. 'Thanks.' He got in, into the back past the tip-up seat. '25 Tilbury, I live.'

'I know, I know,' the man laughed. He put the car into gear and checked carefully in the off-side mirror. '25 Tilbury, it is.'

CHAPTER TWO

Boys do still like sweets?

Rachel Power stood dripping water into a growing pool on the kitchen floor.

'You stupid girl,' her mother said, 'coming in like this. Look at my tiles. You're soaking wet!'

'Well, I couldn't come in dry. It's pouring down with rain!'

'As if I'm not up to my eyes already. Look

at these clothes. Ruined! Do you think money for clothes grows on trees? You could've took shelter, couldn't you?'

'Where?'

'Back in school, for a start.'

'No chance. Them cleaners moan more'n you do!'

Wet smacks hurt worse than dry, and the one Rachel got made her jump and shout as Mrs Power started tugging the clothes over her head.

'You'll remember tonight, my girl!' she said. 'Little madam! You mark my words!'

The car Nicky was in had started to pick up speed. The man was saying nothing, giving everything to the road: kept on looking in his mirrors and peering through the slashing wipers.

Nicky knew driving was hard in this rain,

knew the man had to concentrate; but he also knew they were going much too fast on a road this wet; well, faster than his dad would go, anyway. And there was no sense racing, because he only lived round the corner. He looked past the driver's head and squinted to see the end of his street. At this speed they'd go flying past if they weren't careful.

'It's just down here, next on the right.

'Eh?'

'My street. You know, Tilbury. Look there!' Nicky's voice rose to a shout as the car swished on past his turning at something over forty miles an hour. 'You've missed it. I said . . . Look, go down this next one.'

But the car kept on going, and the man at the wheel looked as if he didn't even want to slow down.

'You've gone past the next one and all!'

'That's all right. Don't get worried, son. I've

just had an idea, that's all. Being wet. A bit of a surprise, something to tell your teacher about, won't take long. Then I'll have you home in no time.'

He had that little laugh in his voice, the one his uncle had when he came in holding something secret behind his back. But what surprise could this bloke have in the rain that wouldn't take five minutes? It didn't sound right, somehow.

'*Where* do you live?' Nicky asked.

'Not far. You must've seen me in the shops, or somewhere. I know you.'

'Do you know my name?' Nicky's voice sounded strange, even to himself; like in a room without an echo.

'Eh? What's that, son?'

That 'son' again. Is that really all he could call him? 'Son' was a label Nicky hated from anyone except his mum and dad.

Meanwhile another side street went by, and another, with the man hunched more and more over his wheel.

'Will you stop now, please? I think I want to get out.'

Nicky leaned over the seat, but the man

only laughed, as if it was all a bit of fun and Nicky just wasn't in on the secret. 'Hey, don't get yourself all het up. I told you, it's a surprise. You'll see. Wouldn't want to spoil it for me, would you?'

'What's my name, then? Just tell me my name, if you know me.' Nicky felt his throat getting tight.

'Don't have to know your name to know you, do I? Do you know the names of all the neighbours in your street?' He gave a quick look round at him and smiled. 'Here, you're not scared of me, are you?' And he laughed again, as if that was something impossible.

'No, but . . .' It seemed a shame to hurt the man's feelings – it was just that they were going further and further away from home, the streets all flashing past in the spray, till this wasn't even the long way round any more.

'I'll tell you what. Have a sweet. Boys do still like sweets, don't they?'

With his free hand the man pulled down the little door of the glove compartment.

Nicky stared. He'd never seen so many packets and bars crammed into such a small space before.

'I've got a sweet tooth, too. There should be something in there you like.'

'Well, just tell me where we're going, then.'

The man banged both his hands on the steering wheel, like Nicky's father did when he was fed up in heavy traffic. 'All right, spoil the surprise.' He took out a Mars Bar and lobbed it into the back. 'Just down to the marshes. Not all that far.'

Which yellow Mini?

Nicky's mother hardly got a word out before
Mrs Power dragged her into the kitchen.
'What do you do with kids like this?' she
asked. 'Look at those clothes! Wouldn't you
credit a girl that age with more sense than to
run home in that storm?'

Rachel stood looking sheepish in her
pyjamas. There was no need to make her

disgrace all public to Nicky's mum.

Mrs Davis stared at the pants, socks and frock heaped up wet in the sink, looking like a little pile of clothing someone might have found out in the open.

'I only wish my Nicky had run home,' she said, 'wet, dry or covered in muck. But I don't know *where* he is, Mrs Power. I've rung the school and they said he came out with your Rachel.' Her eyes begged for some news.

'He's gone in with a mate, love. Found the dry. Always had more up top, your boy. You haven't given him long, have you?'

'It's just, he never does that. He knows . . .'

'He never went in with a mate.' Both the women turned to look at Rachel, who, knowing what Nicky had done, could afford to fold her arms and look smug. 'He went off in his dad's car. His dad picked him up. I saw him.'

'His dad? He can't have.' Mrs Davis frowned. 'The car's laid up, been out the front for a month, and his dad's as much up the wall over him as I am.'

'But I saw it. Yellow Mini, isn't it? I know the colour. Didn't actually see his dad, but I definitely saw Nicky getting in it. I know 'cos I saw the number, would've had a laugh if it

hadn't been so wet . . .' Rachel looked from
one to the other as if they wouldn't under-
stand. 'See, it's a sort of a joke we've got . . .
an' that number . . .'

Mrs Davis grabbed hold of Mrs Power's
arm. 'Could your Rachel throw some things
on and come back with me?' she pleaded.
'Please? Tell Mr Davis all about this car?'

Mrs Power looked a bit put out with
having to release Rachel from her punish-
ment, but she nodded. 'All right, if you like.
Put your mac on, Rachel – and come straight
back. But this had better not be one of your
airy-fairy stories, madam!' The look she gave
to Rachel promised another good smack if it
was. 'We're none of us in the mood for jokes
tonight.'

Once round the corner, the look on Rachel's
face said she wished she'd never seen

anything. Or never said anything about it, anyway.

They were on the Davises' doorstep. Nicky's mother wasn't waiting till they got inside: she grabbed her husband as he opened the door.

'Rachel saw a yellow car. Like ours. Nicky getting into it – and something funny about it.'

'Getting into it?' Mr Davis threw his cigarette into the garden.

'She reckons you picked Nicky up from school just when the rain came on.'

Mr Davis looked at Rachel. 'In that?' He waved at the yellow Mini on the grass. It was sitting up on its blocks with water dripping from where the wheels weren't. 'How could I pick him up in that?'

Rachel stared at the stranded vehicle. She felt awkward now, under attack in a strange way, but with nothing actually being said. At least she knew where she stood with her

mum's hard line. She looked at the rusting bodywork, trying to find something useful to say.

'Well?' There was more than a hint of disbelief in Mr Davis's voice.

'I don't know . . .' But now Rachel looked at

the number plate, dim and dirty, and . . .
'Hey! Yours *is* a different number. The other
one, like I said, it was funny . . . I remember
seeing it . . .' Her mind went back to that
quick look in the rain, that something about
the car number that she'd wanted to tell
someone.

'That other one. It was LEY something.

The same as we're trying to rub off *Bottomley* on the school sign.' She went red, almost ashamed to admit their baby trick of trying to make it say *A Bottom*. 'That's why I noticed it.'

'Nine, nine, nine!' Mrs Davis was pulling hard at her husband's arm. 'Nine, nine, nine!' she shouted.

'I didn't see the number,' said Rachel, 'only LEY.'

'No - nine, nine, nine, *police*!' Mrs Davis ran into the living room. 'Our Nicky's gone off in a car with someone, some stranger!'

But her shaking fingers couldn't find the holes in the telephone, and Nicky's father had to pull it out of her hands and do it for her.

CHAPTER FOUR

Down to the marshes

If the sky had seemed low before, down on the marshes it was close enough to touch. The rain had stopped, but a clam in the air like wet flannels round the face hit Nicky as the car door opened.

His spirits had fallen with the sky.

He'd felt so helpless in the car. Like a bad ride at the fair, it had been, when there was no stopping the roundabout however much you screamed and shouted, because that was what people were supposed to do. Not that Nicky had done that. The last thing he wanted was for the man to think he was scared. But he had wanted the car to stop, and he had wanted to be let out where lots of people were.

Now they were here on the marshes: and all at once the car seemed a safer place to be.

All the way there Nicky had known he couldn't reach the door from the back. Not to get out. His own car was the same. And even if he could, there'd been no stopping any-where, not even at cross roads. The man had seemed to time it so that the car never even slowed down.

Or was all that in Nicky's mind? Was he being all dramatic like his mother sometimes said he was? The man had still sounded gentle and nice. He'd laughed and joked and

kept on giving him sweets. But he wouldn't
say another word about what sort of surprise
he'd got, however many ways Nicky had tried
to ask. They were down by the river now, and
the car had stopped in a farmer's gate. And
all there was to see was sky and water and

marsh: and the only living things were several silly sheep who ran away as soon as the car had stopped.

'Come on, son,' the man said firmly. 'Nearly there. Time to get out.'

Nicky had never felt so alone. No-one came down here to play. Half a mile upstream the bigger boys went fishing, and further down they looked for old bottles. But here it was just boggy marsh all the way to the river, and the old army rifle range in between. Apart from the sheep that was all it was fit for: shooting bullets into things.

The man took Nicky by the wrist and helped him out of the car. 'Come on, over here.'

'Where? Where we going? I want to go home.'

'Don't be daft! Just you wait till you see . . .' The man's raincoat flapped and his wispy hair blew all ways as he bent his body into

the wind and started walking them fast
across the rough, wet ground.

'You stop it! Let me go! I don't want to
come. I want to go home!' Nicky pulled at the
arm and tried to dig his heels in.

'Now don't you be silly. I'll take you home
all right. A surprise I said, didn't I? Well, a
surprise you're going to have. You've come
this far, haven't you?' The man's voice was
raised above the whine of the marsh wind as
he gripped Nicky's wrist harder and pulled
him on again.

'Let go! You're hurting!' But Nicky's voice
hardly reached his own ears.

'Stupid, you'll get lost out here if you run.
Come on, nearly there.' The man was shouting,
pointing with his free hand and pulling him
hard towards the lines of soldiers' trenches.
And now Nicky knew for sure. The man *was*
one of those they warned you about. He'd

got hold of him too hard, his voice was too rough – and he was pulling him towards the trenches. What proper surprise could anyone have down there?

'Stop it! *Stop*! Let me go!'

Nicky twisted his wrist to get out of the grip. He bit at the big sleeve, kicked at the long legs – but the man's strong grip didn't loosen, and he was being half-pulled and half-carried towards the second trench.

'You wanna get lost? Now you stop all that!' the man snapped. 'Or you'll start getting me cross, boy!'

Nicky looked at him with wide, terrified eyes: because now a new face went with the new voice, and all the man's pretence at niceness had gone.

Two policemen filled the small front room like grown-ups in a home corner.

'How did you know my son lived here?' the old lady asked them. 'He's never had any dealings with the police before.'

'On the computer, radio'd through to us. A bit of his number plate and the make of his car. It is your son's car, isn't it?'

'It must be if you say it is. Why, what's he supposed to have done?'

44

One of the policemen sat in a chair. 'Nothing, missus, if we're in time . . .'

'. . . If you can help us find him, quick. Like, are there any favourite places he goes to . . . ?'

The old lady frowned and touched the tea-pot no-one had time for. 'Well, if he's not at work . . .'

'He's not at work.'

'Then the only place he goes is bird watching. He loves it, he's quite an expert. He'd spend his life there if he could.'

'Where, love, where?'

Nobody blinked.

'Down on the marshes. By the old range. Wonderful sights, he's seen down there . . .'

But as she drew breath to tell them of those wonders, the race began: an obstacle over the chairs to the door, and a head-down sprint to the police car in the street.

CHAPTER FIVE

Run for it!

'Ouch!' Nicky pretended to fall. It was the last trick he knew to play. 'My ankle!' What the mother birds did, the broken wing: something he'd read in a book somewhere.

'Come on, sonny! Stop playing me up.'

The man was really angry now and trying to pull him down into one of the trenches, well out of sight of the road. Which meant

Nicky had only one last possible chance. Stay up here on the flat, if he could . . .

'I can't go no further. I've broke my ankle.' He sank with all his weight on one side to the ground.

'Come on, get up, who d'you think you're kidding?'

The man tugged at him; but with Nicky on the ground he had to alter his feet, shift his grip, let go for half a second. And, suddenly, there was the chance. Like 'releaso'! A life-time's practice in the playground suddenly paid off. Nicky dug in his toes, and pushed, and ran for his life away from the man's reach and towards the river. He put down his head and thrust all his energy into his clammy, wet legs.

And all the man did was laugh. A low and throaty laugh which even the wind couldn't get at. I'll catch you, it seemed to say, I'll catch

you, son. There's no getting away from me.

But Nicky tried. He stumbled and tripped on the hillocky ground, he whipped his face in the reed-grass, his ankle went over for real. But he ran as the laugh came after him, and he kept on running after the laugh had stopped. Cold marsh air filled his lungs, and his throat burned hotter than hell. Wind seared his eyes as he stared at the river, a hammer seemed to thud at his heart. He was going the wrong way, he knew he was: the wrong way, away from the gate and the road.

But getting away from the man came first! Away anywhere. Into a cluster of thin bushes. Zig-zag in and out, keep them between him and the man, dodge and run. He grabbed a prickly handful out of his way and looked for him. There was no sign. The marsh behind him was as dead as the moon. And there was the nearest trench: twenty metres away: get round the end of that and away up the other side and then the man could get lost – *he'd* be back at the road!

A quick last look. All clear still. Had the bloke given up when he saw the run Nicky had in him? Please, Mum, yes! Then leg it for home! To the end of that trench – and round it – now!

Nicky spurted – and suddenly sprang into the air in terror as a loud footstep splashed centimetres behind him and hard breathing wheezed close to his head.

'Come here, you young fool!'

God! He was . . . ! How could . . . !? Without thinking, Nicky threw his body forward, jerked his head to his waist to avoid the clutch. Help! Could he still make it to the other side of the trench and turn the chase – bolt for the road before the maniac got him?

Nicky shut his eyes. A last desperate push, away from those hands –.

And down! All at once his feet had gone from under him and he was doing a mad dance in space, clutching at nothing, dirt in his mouth – landing with a sickening thud to sprawl flat in the bottom of an overgrown slit trench. He was winded, stunned, his chest hurt and he had to claw mud from his eyes.

But he stumbled to his feet. He had to keep
going, he knew. There were no second chances in this deadly game of chase. But which
way was he facing? Which way to go now?

Who cared which way? Just run! He
banged and grazed himself on the crumbling
wall. Sheer panic drove him on along the
trench.

But he heard the thump as the man dropped down behind him: down here where no-one would see them. Just where he'd wanted him! And then the footsteps again, heavy, determined to get him.

But there was an end to the trench. Nicky could see it. If he could get there in time, climb out before . . .

The black mud favoured light feet, and for those last few seconds Nicky thought he had just the ghost of a chance – if he could only climb far enough up that trench end to kick at the hands which'd grab at his legs.

One last effort! There'd never be another chance, not ever in his life. The end of the trench was the end of the chase.

Nicky got there, shut his ears to what was coming as he leapt at the soil, scrambled like an animal to the rim above his head. He put his life on every thin blade of grass fingers could find. He kicked. He scrabbled. He screamed at where he wanted to be as if screaming would somehow get him there.

And then he saw it. Above him. Looming above. The big black shape. The man! Who'd got out, gone round, cut him off.

'No!' yelled Nicky. 'No! You . . . !'

CHAPTER SIX

Your guess is as good as mine

The hand grabbing down was big and wet.
But there was never any chance of slipping
that grip. The time for slips and mistakes was
over.

'Come on, my son, I've got you,' the policeman said: and that 'my son' was the most
welcome sound in all the world to Nicky.
'You're a lucky little devil, I'll tell you!'

He was lifted out to the sound of shouting back in the trench – of which Nicky heard nothing as he heaved for breath and stood shaking with the end of his efforts.

All the way across the hundred metres of stumbling footsteps, over to the road and the

cars clustered round the yellow Mini, Nicky kept himself dry-eyed and dignified in the policeman's arms: right up to the moment he saw his parents drive up. And then everyone seemed to cry, and a word was as hard to get out as a hair in the mouth. But out it came in the end. The relief, the thanks to sharp-eyed Rachel, to the police computer and the speed of a radio-controlled car. And then, because they had to be said, a few soft words of reproach.

'You should never have done it, Nicky.'

'Never go off with *anyone*. How many times have we told you?'

'It doesn't matter *what* they say.'

'There are more sick people about than there are bolts of lightning heading for you. You should've gone back in school, Nicky. There are people you can trust there.'

Nicky nodded. There was no excuse. He'd

been stupid, he knew that – and a lucky little
devil, like the policeman said.

'You know what his story was?' Nicky's
father asked.

'No?' Nicky put a thumb in his book. He
wanted to know. He'd had a bad time, but he
could cope with talking about it now – here
in the safety of his bedroom where all that

had happened seemed so unreal.

'He reckons he had a nest to show you. Something any kid would give his eye-teeth to see, he said. A heron's or something, down on the river's edge: very rare, on the ground, with the mother on her eggs in the rain.'

'Do they believe him?'

'He showed them the nest, all right. And back home he's got binoculars and books on it, and everything.'

Nicky closed his eyes. He tried to go back over what had happened: tried to remember exactly what had been said. It was true he hadn't been threatened, except with getting lost. He hadn't been *told* anything, and nothing had actually been *done* to him, had it? So had it just been him? Had he been scared out of his life for nothing? Would it all have been all right if he hadn't panicked and run?

He didn't think so.

He opened his eyes again and looked at his dad.

'Do *you* believe him? Do you reckon he was . . . going to . . . you know?'

Mr Davis sat silent for a moment. '*I* don't know,' he said. He looked at the spy story Nicky was holding. 'Life's a lot more complicated than that sort of thing makes out, you know. Like, has it struck you that guy doesn't even know himself what he was going to do . . . ?'

Nicky stared at his dad: somehow, that made it all sound even worse, the man not knowing, acting no different to some kid.

'No, mate, I couldn't tell you. And the chances are, he couldn't, either. What's certain is that social services know about him now. If he needs some help he's in the right hands. But as for today – your guess is as good as mine . . '

Nicky shivered: slid down into his bed. This wasn't the way it should have been, this not being sure, this still feeling jumpy. There was only one thing for it: get the light out, get to sleep, quick, get today over and done with. And keep his fingers crossed that the only jumps he had tomorrow would be the ones he wanted – up at the L E Y of *Bottomley* on the school sign.

All About Barn Owl Books

If you've ever scoured the bookshops for that book you loved as a child or the one your children wanted to hear again and again and been frustrated then you'll know why Barn Owl Books exists. We are hoping to bring back many of the excellent books that have slipped from publishers' backlists in the last few years.

Barn Owl is devoted entirely to reprinting worthwhile out-of-print children's books. Initially we will not be doing any picture books, purely because of the high costs involved, but any other kind of children's book will be considered. We are always on the lookout for new titles and hope that the public will help by letting us know what their own special favourites are. If anyone would like to photocopy and fill in the form below giving us their suggestions for future titles we would be delighted. We do hope that you enjoyed this book and will read our other Barn Owl titles.

Books I would like to see back in print include:

Name

Address

Please return to Ann Jungman, Barn Owl Books
15 New Cavendish Street, London W1M 7AL

Barn Owl Books

THE PUBLISHING HOUSE DEVOTED ENTIRELY TO
THE REPRINTING OF CHILDREN'S BOOKS

RECENT TITLES

The Spiral Stair – Joan Aiken
Giraffe thieves are about! Arabel and her raven have to act fast

Voyage – Adèle Geras
Story of four young Russians sailing to the US in 1904

Private – Keep Out! – Gwen Grant
Diary of the youngest of six in the 1940s

Leila's Magical Monster Party – Ann Jungman
Leila invites all the worst baddies to her party and they come!

The Mustang Machine – Chris Powling
A magic bike sorts out the bullies

You're thinking about doughnuts – Michael Rosen
Frank is left alone in a scary museum at night

Jimmy Jelly – Jacqueline Wilson
A T.V. personality is confronted by his greatest fan